HIGH SCHOOL MUSICAL 3 SENIOR YEAR

TAKE A BOW

Adapted by Lara Bergen

Based on the screenplay written by Peter Barsocchini

Based on characters created by Peter Barsocchini

Executive Producer Kenny Ortega

Produced by Bill Borden and Barry Rosenbush

Directed by Kenny Ortega

DISNEP PRESS

New York

Copyright © 2009 Disney Enterprises, Inc.
All rights reserved. Published by Disney Press, an imprint of Disney Book Group.
No part of this book may be reproduced or transmitted in any form or by any means,
electronic or mechanical, including photocopying, recording, or by any information
storage and retrieval system, without written permission from the publisher. For
information address Disney Press, 114 Fifth Avenue, New York, New York 10011-5690.
Printed in the United States of America

First Edition

1 3 5 7 9 10 8 6 4 2

Library of Congress Control Number: 2008903897

ISBN 978-1-4231-1206-8

For more Disney Press fun, visit www.disneybooks.com
Visit disney.com/HSM3

Life was good for Troy Bolton, Gabriella Montez, and the rest of their friends. They were seniors. They ruled East High. And they were all going to make their last semester the best ever!

Still, the Wildcats weren't sure if they really had time to participate in another musical. Jason Cross had to study for finals. Zeke Baylor had recipes to perfect. And Taylor McKessie had a whole yearbook to edit. "Sorry, no can do," she said.

But then Gabriella spoke up. "This is our last chance to do something together, all of us. Something really fun," she told them. Besides, they just *had* to be in the musical. After all, it was about the seniors!

As Ms. Darbus, the drama teacher, explained, "The spring musical will be called *Senior Year*!" And that wasn't the only exciting news Ms. Darbus had. The Juilliard School in New York City was considering four seniors for a scholarship: Sharpay Evans; her twin brother, Ryan; Kelsi Nielsen; and . . . Troy!

"But I've never even heard of Juilliard," Troy admitted to Ms. Darbus. Plus, he already had a basketball scholarship to the University of Albuquerque lined up. How, Troy wondered, had the Juilliard School heard of him?

Sharpay wondered the exact same thing. She figured Troy was just pretending not to know.

"Performers can't fool me," she told Ryan.

"But there's only *one* scholarship," Ryan reminded her.

"We're twins," Sharpay told him. "They'll have to take us both."

CHAPTER 2

Luckily, Sharpay had someone who could help Ryan and her win the Juilliard scholarship—her own personal assistant and understudy, Tiara Gold, a new transfer student from London, England.

A few days later, Tiara overheard Gabriella and Taylor talking in the yearbook committee room. Gabriella had just gotten a letter from Stanford University. They had offered her a place in their freshman honors program.

But Gabriella didn't look that happy. So Tiara did some snooping.

It seemed that the honors program was a three-week-long event that started before senior year was over.

"It means she'd miss our . . . I mean *your* . . . show," Tiara told Sharpay.

"Well!" exclaimed Sharpay with a wide grin. That was certainly the best news she'd heard all day.

"The show must go on . . . mustn't it?" Sharpay asked Tiara.

Sharpay knew that without Gabriella there, *she* could sing her songs and be the true star of the show. (And Tiara knew that if that happened, *she* could fill Sharpay's shoes!)

Still, Sharpay was afraid of the one thing that could keep Gabriella from going: Troy. She cornered him at his locker the next day.

"Congratulations!" she told him. When he looked surprised, she explained about the honors program.

"I guess Gabriella not telling you means she's on the fence about it," said Sharpay. "But who better than Troy Bolton to encourage her to accept . . . since the only thing holding her back is probably . . . you."

"Of course, you should go," Troy told Gabriella later that night. It was an amazing opportunity, and he didn't want her to miss it. But he knew Gabriella wanted senior year to last forever.

"But we're going to graduate," Troy told her. "That's going to happen, no matter what."

CHAPTER 3

Gabriella packed her bags and left for Stanford the next week. But back at East High, things weren't the same without her. Except for Sharpay and Tiara, everyone missed Gabriella. They tried to rehearse for the musical, but their hearts just weren't in it. Especially Troy's.

Troy had a lot on his mind. Finally, he went to the one place where he knew he could think—the East High auditorium. Troy was surprised to find Ms. Darbus there, too.

"I know I'm not supposed to be here," he said.

"Aren't you?" she asked. "Nor am I, I suppose. But the stage is a great partner in self-discovery, and you seem very comfortable up there . . . which is why I submitted your name to Juilliard."

"It was you?" Troy wasn't mad . . . just confused.

"Better to consider opportunities now, than in ten years when life might limit your choices," she explained. "If I've overstepped, I'm sorry."

Troy thought about what Ms. Darbus had said. He then made an important decision about college, and his future. He knew exactly what he had to do next.

CHAPTER 4

The very next day, which was the day of the East High prom, Troy drove up to Stanford to surprise Gabriella. They danced around the quad.

"You may be ready to say good-bye to East High," Troy told Gabriella, "but East High isn't ready to say good-bye to you."

Gabriella wasn't ready to say good-bye to East High, either. And even though Troy and Gabriella knew they could never get back in time for the prom, they still might be able to participate in the spring musical. If they hurried, maybe, just maybe, they could make the second act!

In the meantime, the spring musical would have to go on without them . . . with the understudies stepping in for the missing leads. Sharpay would play Gabriella's part, Tiara would act out Sharpay's role, and sophomore Jimmie "the Rocket" Zara would stand in for Troy.

Ms. Darbus had decided to make Jimmie Troy's understudy because he really admired the Wildcats' captain. It was Jimmie's first year on the basketball team, and he wanted to be like Troy in every way. But he'd never understood what "understudy" meant . . . until then. He was petrified.

"Get him oxygen!" Ms. Darbus yelled. "It's showtime!"

CHAPTER 5

Unfortunately, no amount of oxygen could clear the air of Jimmie's horrible cologne. As soon as he came close to Sharpay, she started sneezing.

Sharpay's big chance to impress the Juilliard scouts was turning out to be a disaster!

Luckily, Gabriella and Troy arrived to take Jimmie's and Sharpay's places. They sang the special song that Kelsi had written for them, and the audience cheered loudly. The musical was saved!

Sharpay stormed back to her dressing room to prepare for the part she was originally going to play. But a big surprise was waiting. Tiara was wearing a fancy blue dress and sitting in Sharpay's makeup chair!

"I'm playing Sharpay, remember?" Tiara said as she headed for the stage. "Step aside. I need to warm up and make a good impression since it will be *my* drama department next year."

But "aside" was not a direction in which Sharpay liked to step.

"If East High is going to remember one
Sharpay," she declared, "it's going to be ME!"
And she followed Tiara onto the stage for a duel
of the East High divas no one would ever forget.

CHAPTER 6

After the spring musical was over, that meant it would soon be time for graduation and the exciting news about two of East High's talented seniors. Juilliard had made their decision, and just as Sharpay had predicted, they *were* going to give two scholarships that year, but she wasn't one of their choices. The scholarships were offered to Ryan and Kelsi!

But Sharpay wasn't all that disappointed. Ms. Darbus had already asked her to run the drama department while she took a leave for the fall semester. Sharpay would get to direct all the musicals and be in charge of running the Drama Club. For Sharpay, it was *another* dream come true!

Even Troy had surprising news to share. He'd made a decision about college—he'd chosen basketball *and* theater.

He would be going to the University of California in Berkeley. It had both things he loved—and it was just thirty miles from Stanford!

And who knew what other dreams would come true for the East High Wildcats? One thing was for sure: no matter where the future took them, their memories of East High would stay with them forever!